Whispers of the Beyond

By Cade Sneed

To my wife Alexis, who is my muse, my confidante, and my greatest supporter.

Author's Note

Because of the heavy nature of the short stories you will find within this novel, I've decided to provide a forewarning. The following content may cause discomfort or be triggering to some readers, as this book contains graphic mentions of suicide, drug use, and homicide.

This book, in contrast to many narratives you may encounter, does not romanticize pain. There is nothing romantic in tragedy. Rather, it is something that we must all deal with in life, and something that we mustn't let define us.

These stories draw inspiration from the raw emotions of those I've encountered on my journey through life. The grief of a lost love, the anguish of knowing you cannot save a drowning friend, and the struggle to forgive even when it goes against everything within you-- these are the emotional landscapes explored within these pages.

Eternal Echoes

"Let's get this over with," growled a deep voice. I opened my eyes and the room materialized in a blurry dance of shadows and uncertain shapes. *What was happening?*

I inhaled deeply, attempting to piece together the fragmented memories. The last coherent image was a swig of Jameson on the cold tile of my bathroom floor. And then… nothing. No matter how hard I tried, I couldn't remember any further than that.

"Name and date of birth?" The gravelly voice said, cutting through the disarray of my thoughts. Seated across from me was a silhouette cloaked in a pitch black robe. I glanced around, realizing I seemed to be inside of an empty warehouse, seated at a folding table across from this mysterious individual.

"Hey!" the figure's knuckles wrapped sharply on the table, jolting me back to the present. "Kid! Name and date of birth! I don't have all day."

I swallowed, attempting to refocus on this enigmatic encounter. "Umm… I'm Carter. My birthdate is 3/10/1984." I met the inscrutable gaze of the figure. "Listen man, I'm not sure how I got here, but I'm pretty certain I don't want to be a part of whatever the hell it is you're doing here, so I think I'm just going to go now." Rising hastily, I scanned the dimly lit space for an exit, my senses tingling with a blend of trepidation and curiosity.

"There's no way out of here, kid. You're in the Halfway now. But it's good to know I've got the right person here. I wouldn't want any accidents like last time. Boy there was a lot of paperwork trying to sort that out!" He gave a low chuckle. "Come on kid, sit back down for a minute. We have a lot to talk about." I slowly lowered myself back into my seat, an uneasy feeling creeping into my gut.

"So this is it," the man said. "I hate to be the bearer of bad news Carter, but I'm afraid I'll have to be the one to tell you that you're dead."

I sat in stunned silence for a moment. This man was crazy. He had to be! Or maybe I was. After all, I was sitting across from a man dressed like the Grim Reaper in the middle of some abandoned building, and I hadn't even considered calling 911 yet.

I reached for my cell phone, usually in the front left pocket of my jeans. However, it was nowhere to be found. "What did you do with my phone?" I demanded.

The man shrugged. "Those things don't come with you when you die. Until 100 years ago, neither did your clothes, but I launched a complaint with the man upstairs about that one. Now you just come wearing what you died in."

"You're crazy!" I exclaimed and stood again. Dead? There was no way! To my right glowed a neon 'Exit' sign, and I let out a sigh of

relief. A way out! I headed towards the door

and threw it open, stepping forward before

quickly retracting at the sight of what lay beyond

the door. Because outside was… well… the

universe.

Stars glowed in every direction, and the

outline of a planet could be seen looming in the

far distance. This couldn't be happening! My

breath quickened as my heart pounded against

my chest. Was I really… no, I couldn't be. But

then, like a tidal wave crashing against a

cliffside, it all came back to me. The car

accident. The phone call. The pills.

Hot tears burned my eyes, leaving salty

trails down my face. It was undeniable; I was

dead.

"Why don't you sit back down,Carter,"

came a gentle voice from beside me. The man

grasped my shoulders and led me delicately back

to my seat. I sobbed for a few moments, the

man offering silent solace as I wept.

"Are you the Grim Reaper?" I finally asked once my sobs had subdued. I tried to steady my voice, but despite my best efforts it shook with fear.

"People usually call me Grim," The figure responded with a hint of wryness, "But you can call me whatever you like. I've heard all the names. Hel, Thanatos, Shinigami, and just about every moniker for death you could possibly think of."

I nodded in acknowledgement. "Grim," I said, my voice still tinged with emotion. "I'll just call you Grim."

He tilted his head in agreement. "Well, Carter," Grim began. "I'll be your tour guide through the Halfway. This is the area between life and death; the place where you're not quite dead yet, but you aren't quite alive either. From this point it's entirely up to you what happens. Some people choose to continue into death, or what I like to call the Unknown, but many people return to Earth and forget these

encounters ever happened. The choice is yours.
I'm merely here to help you make the decision."

His speech carried a hint of boredom, as if
he had recited this spiel countless times before,
navigating the liminal space between life and
whatever lay beyond.

"Grim," I interrupted, a newfound
boldness infusing my words. "If we're going to
be… like… talking or something, would you
mind losing the cloak? The whole 'Reaper of
Death' thing kind of creeps me out.

He stared at me for a moment, and though I couldn't see his face, I sensed his surprise at my unusual request.

"You know," he said quietly, "Out of all my centuries of doing this, you're the first person to ever ask me that. Usually people are too afraid to see what's underneath this whole getup."

I shrugged. A mix of emotions were indeed swirling within me, but fear wasn't among them. I had heard gruesome tales of a reaper with skin peeled from face, exposed eye sockets, and maggots covering a bony skeleton. And while I wasn't particularly eager to witness such a sight, a morbid curiosity stirred within me.

"I'm not afraid" I declared, establishing an agreement that I would bear the responsibility for whatever horrors lay beneath-- After all, it wasn't as though I could die of fright, was it?

Grim pushed back his sleeves to reveal calloused hands and thin arms. Then, with deliberate slowness, he lowered his hood. To my surprise, he looked like an average eighty year-old man. In fact, the only thing that would have separated him from anyone else in a retirement home were his eyes, which bore a wild, haunted look.

As I gazed into his ocean-colored eyes, a pang of sympathy washed over me. I understood that haunted look all too well. It was the stare of a man who had seen too much; who had been broken by the weight of death. I had seen that same look every time I gazed into my reflection since the accident.

"I have to say, I was expecting a little more gore," I said lightly, and he smiled at me. It was a thin smile that didn't reach his eyes.

"What's more death-like than old age, kid?" He asked me. "Everybody's gotta age eventually. Some of us die a little younger, like in your case, but the rest of us, we lose control of our legs and our bowels and we go out pissing ourselves cause we can't reach the bathroom. Death and old age go hand in hand," He linked his fingers together for effect, emphasizing the inexorable connection between life's final chapter and the passage of time.

Before I had a chance to conjure a response, Grim pressed on. "Now, on with the important stuff. You know you're dead. You know where you're at. Now on to your last viewing. Where do you want to go?"

I stared at him blankly.

"Your last viewing," he repeated patiently. "Think of it as an opportunity to watch any one of your greatest moments in life. Maybe you won some prize or held your child for the first time. Choose a good one, because after that, you might choose to pass into the Unknown.

"Wait" I said slowly, trying to wrap my head around the concept. "So I just choose any moment in my life that I want to play back, and then I get to see it?"

"Bingo," Grim winked. It struck me as unsettling how light his demeanor remained, despite the gravity of the situation.

"Rules are the same for everybody. You get up to 10 minutes of viewing time. After that you make your decision of where to go. No crying or whining or begging for more time. So go ahead and choose a memory. When you've got one locked in, concentrate on it hard, and it'll materialize around us."

The prospect of reliving a cherished moment felt like a bittersweet gift. A brief respite in the limbo between life and whatever lay beyond. Still, I already knew I'd be passing on after I watched my memory, so I suppose it didn't really matter which one I chose. Or maybe, I considered, this fact only made the choosing more significant. This would be my last chance to see the world through my own

eyes.

What, out of everything that I had done in

my small and insignificant life, was worth seeing

again?

I pondered all that I had done. The sale

that brought about a policy change and

commission cap at the office. The times I spent

volunteering at the homeless shelter. The best

meals I ate and the funniest jokes I heard. What,

of all of those moments, was worth reliving? As

I considered, my mind settled on a memory

I closed my eyes closed tight, immersing myself in the recollection of the aroma of fresh baked bread and the harmonious melody of laughter. When I opened my eyes again, my surroundings had transformed. The building around me had morphed into the kitchen at my first apartment, with floral wallpaper peeling above the fridge, and a freshly baked loaf of cinnamon bread steaming on the countertop. This was home. Which meant…

I heard the laughter first. *His* laughter. "Carter!" He sang, flouncing into the kitchen.

"You'd better hurry up because I *will* eat this entire loaf of bread by myself! You know I love this stuff!" My husband was just as I remembered him, with a scrappy beard and obnoxious purple fingernails. God, I had hated those fingernails. But now… now I would do anything just to see him paint them again.

"I'm coming, dear!" I heard my own voice call from the living room. A younger version of me walked into the kitchen, grinning. "Cut me a slice, Oliver. And don't forget to return the neighbor's pan tomorrow. I'll never hear the end of it if Mrs. Jackson doesn't get it back."

Young Carter's smile was infectious, and I felt tears welling up in my eyes once more. I could not remember the last time I had smiled like that.

"I'll return the pan, honey," Oliver promised younger me. Then, he leaned in for a kiss.

"Who is that?" Grim asked from beside me, causing me to jump. For a moment I had forgotten he was there. For a moment the only people in the world were me and Oliver.

I took a deep breath. "That's my partner,"
I told him quietly. "His name was Oliver. He
was wonderful. I always told him he was the
best thing that ever happened to me." The weight
of nostalgia hung in the air as the scene
unfolded; a cherished memory that had become a
poignant testament to a life that once was.

Grim nodded solemnly. "I'm sure he'll
miss you if you pass into the Unknown."

I bit my lip as the tears trickled down my
cheeks. "He… um… he passed away last week.

A year ago we were driving home from the grocery store and we were hit by a drunk driver. I only broke my arm, but he… um… well, he ended up on life support and never got better. I'll never forget the call I got the day he passed. The nurses knew me by name." I took a deep, shaky breath and looked away, wiping my face on the sleeve of my shirt.

Grim reached out and put a hand softly on my shoulder. "I'm sorry," he said, and I could tell that he meant it.

"Me too," I whispered. "I couldn't live

without him."

I watched as young Carter and Oliver sat

together at the worn kitchen table, cutting slices

of bread and feeding them to each other while

laughing about work and television, and

anything else that they pleased. I felt envy burn

within me. I wished, desperately, to go back to

those days, sitting by the side of my soulmate

and laughing because we were young and life

was sweet. But those days were long gone.

"It's time." Grim said finally. The kitchen slowly faded into darkness until we were shrouded in black. Then, as though someone had flipped on a light switch, the room once again illuminated, resuming its original appearance as a warehouse.

We sat in silence for a moment before Grim cleared his throat. "So, Carter, I now offer you two choices. The first, and most popular, is to return to the living. Many choose this option simply because, while their bodies are broken and old, they fear the Unknown. Take, for instance, an elderly woman on a ventilator.

Should she choose to stay, she would be sent back into her body where she would live, stuck inside a shell and forced to wait until I come back for her again." Grim shuddered.

"One could question whether this option even counts as living… but I offer it nonetheless. Luckily, it looks like in your case," he consulted his notes, "your body is actually in quite a suitable condition at the moment. The doctors are optimistic that you could awaken from your coma soon. Although it doesn't say how you managed to make it here if you're doing so well… but nonetheless, returning to

Earth seems like an appropriate option for you to take."

"The road less traveled," he continued, "is to embrace the uncertainty and to enter the Unknown. Of course, that would put an end to your time on Earth. If you choose to take this option, I will put in a request for transport, a boat will arrive at the door you tried to go through earlier, and you will sail off into the stars into what comes next. It's all very ominous."

I opened my mouth, but Grim cut me off. "Don't even bother asking what happens beyond the boat," he said shortly. "The man upstairs says that's none of my business. 'Above my paygrade' apparently."

I nodded politely. Grim's quarrel with whatever god controlled the afterlife was the least of my concerns at the moment.

"I want to go into the Unknown," I told him firmly. He stared at me with disbelief for a moment.

"You… but… I did tell you about the boat, right? Don't you think that's a little creepy? Wouldn't you much rather return to the real world, where you can… I don't know… play with kittens and eat ice cream? Surely you don't want to give it all up in a gamble for whatever comes next," Grim exclaimed in disbelief.

I took a deep breath. "I'm sure," I responded simply. I had made up my mind before I even arrived here.

Grim stared at me for a moment, though I had long ago mastered the art of making my face unreadable. Slowly a look of understanding dawned on Grim's face as he considered all that he had learned about me during our short encounter.

"I suppose I never asked you," he said to me softly, "how you almost died."

"I don't want to talk about that." I responded immediately. He didn't know. He *couldn't* know. But the memories came flooding back. Downing all the whiskey in the cabinet.

The bitter taste of pills on my tongue followed by the violent heaving as my body tried to rid itself of the poisons I had poured carelessly down my throat. The sound of the ambulance outside as I drifted in and out of consciousness.

The memories came pouring back, and the tears had begun to flow again, hot and thick. I couldn't stop myself from crying once more, and this time it felt as though I wouldn't stop.

"How did you get here, Carter?" Grim asked again gently.

"I… I couldn't live without him." I sobbed. "Oliver was the love of my life and now he's gone and… I just couldn't live without him."

Grim shook his head empathetically as it all spilled out of me.

"We were supposed to have time-- 60 years at least. We were supposed to grow gray hair together and get a dog and travel to Scotland and watch shitty movies and get into stupid fights. We were supposed to live our lives together. But now we can't. And I can't do it without him. So yeah, maybe I tried to kill myself, but who wouldn't want to die when their reason for living is ripped away from them?" The raw pain of the confession hung heavy in the air, an unspoken understanding passing between me and Grim in that moment.

"That's a hell of a loss to deal with so young, kid." Grim said quietly. And with that we sat in silence for what felt like forever. But it didn't matter, because what is time to a dead man?

Finally my sobs subdued to sniffles, and I felt my shoulders straighten.

"There's one thing I gotta say, kid." Grim told me. "One thing, and then I'll let you make your choice. And I'll honor whatever you choose to do."

I nodded my agreement.

"What you've been through is something I wouldn't wish on my worst enemy. But how you're feeling right now… you're not special."

I blinked in shock. I had heard

everything, from 'I'm sorry for your loss', to

'You and your boyfriend deserve to rot in hell,

faggot', and yet Grim's comment had been the

first one to truly catch me off guard.

"A million people die on Earth every

day," Grim continued, "and a million more are

left to grieve them. You're not the first suicide

I've seen, kid, and you certainly won't be my

last. But one day you're going to have a

daughter, or a dog, or a friend, and they need

you to be alive right now just like they'll need

you to be alive then. And if you end things right

now, the only thing you guarantee is that they won't have you around when they need you, or even worse, they won't exist because you don't exist!" He sighed and shook his head, his eyes full of sympathy.

"It's not easy when you feel like you've lost your reason to live. But if you stick around, you're going to find another reason. And you're going to heal. And every day is going to get a little easier than the last until you finally feel like you can breathe again."

Grim paused, collecting his thoughts. I could tell he'd had this conversation many times before. I wondered how often it had worked.

"I guess what I'm trying to say, kid, is that miracles happen everyday. And sometimes that miracle is a blind man gaining sight. But sometimes that miracle is just living because everything that hurt you didn't break you, and because you've got someone special who's already passed and who you're determined to make proud. You're one of the lucky ones. Your body isn't too far gone yet. You still have a chance to wake up and see another sunrise."

He cleared his throat, his voice raw with emotion. "A lot of people who attempt don't get the opportunity to go back. Their bodies are too beat up or broken. So before you make the choice to pass on, I want you to think long and hard about what you want to do. I want you to consider if it's really time to throw in the towel, or if you've got even one more day of fight left in you."

Grim shrugged. "I don't know, kid, take it with a grain of salt if you want to. But that's just my two cents."

As Grim's words echoed in my mind, I couldn't shake the weight of his perspective. He spoke of healing; of the gradual easing of pain until the simple act of breathing became a relief. Miracles, he said, sometimes came in the act of staying alive.

But did I believe in miracles? Could I summon the strength to face another day on Earth? To navigate a future without the love that once fueled my existence? As I stood on the precipice of my decision, the question remained:

did I possess the strength to fight for one more

sunrise? One more chance at happiness?

"I've made my decision," I decided. "I'm

going to-"

His Idea of Fun

The buzzer sounded, a sharp and abrasive noise that cut through the air, jolting me into action. The metallic echo resonated as I swung open the heavy door, revealing the parloir beyond. As I stepped inside, a wave of familiarity washed over me, the scene unfolding just like those in every crime drama and prison movie from my childhood.

The parloir, with its cold metal chairs arranged in a stark formation, seemed frozen in time. Grimy wall-mounted phones loomed above, each tethered to its designated seat by a

tangled web of wires. A thick window pane, a

tangible symbol of division, separated the two

realms coexisting within these walls -- one of

freedom, the other of captivity. The thought of a

solitary set of glass standing between the free

and incarcerated added to the unsettling feel of

the room.

Taking a seat at the phone stationed

furthest from the door, I felt the throb of my

heart quicken in anticipation. Nearly two weeks

had passed since I had seen my old friend

Tortoise, and my stomach twisted itself in knots

as an anxious curiosity gripped me. I couldn't

help but wonder if he now regretted the

decisions he had made on the day of the race.

The gravity of the situation weighed on me, and

I considered how easily our lives had diverged,

leading my childhood friend to the confines of

this institution.

Another metallic scraping sound jarred me

from my thoughts, and my friend shuffled over

to the chair across the glass. He looked the same

as he had when I last saw him, with the

exception of his grimy orange jumpsuit and the

heavy dark bags beneath his eyes. As he slumped into the chair opposite mine, the stark reality of his altered state became painfully apparent.

Tortoise's hand trembled slightly as he picked up his phone, and he slowly raised his eyes to meet mine.

"Hare. You came." His once vibrant voice now echoed with a hollow timbre, a departure from the man I once knew.

Our friends had playfully bestowed the nickname 'Tortoise' upon him in grade school; a nod to his nonchalant and deliberate manner of speech. However, this characteristic, once an endearing quirk, now loomed more prominently as another sign that he was still using.

In spite of the grim circumstances, I mustered a feeble smile. My friend was still alive, though the veracity of that statement hung in the air like an unspoken question mark.

"How are you doing in here, man?" I ventured, my voice carrying a blend of concern and guilt.

"Did you get the money I sent you? I know I couldn't send much, but I did what I could." The words tumbled out, accompanied by a pang of remorse as I recalled how long it had taken me to send him anything at all.

He nodded in acknowledgement, his eyes betraying the weariness that extended beyond the physical confines of his cell.

"Thanks for doing what you could, buddy" he replied, his gratitude tempered by the harsh reality of the last several weeks.

"I managed to get some toothpaste from the commissary. Good thing to know my teeth won't go to shit like the rest of me." His attempt at humor, underscored by a dark chuckle, momentarily transported me back to a time when laughter came more easily between us.

It was a fleeting glimpse of how our relationship used to be. The days when we would sit on the back porch of my old apartment, chain-smoking cigarettes and cursing about relationships and the government and everything else that pissed us off. The contrast between then and now left a heavy air between us, an unspoken acknowledgement of the toll that time and circumstance had exacted on both of us.

The nostalgia hit me like a wave, accompanied by a yearning so potent it felt like a physical ache. God, what I wouldn't give to return to those days. When cigarettes were all he would smoke. But time had proven unforgiving, and the simplicity of those

moments had slipped through our fingers.

Cigarettes had turned to blow and dope,

and crack, and whatever else he could get his

hands on, and with that change my friend had

become a mere shell of the man he used to be.

When he first started using, we tried to get

him help. There was a collective effort in our

friend group to rally support and scrape together

enough funds to take him to a treatment center,

but he put up one hell of a fight. So much of a

fight, in fact, that he put a fist-sized hole in the wall of my living room.

The collateral damage came in the form of my lost security deposit, and in the aftermath of that confrontation, an uneasy truce settled in. We didn't talk about treatment anymore, and he didn't break anything else besides himself.

Tortoise unraveled in solitude, and while the rest of us moved forward with life, he remained stagnant. Eventually, each success from one of our friends marked a reminder of the chasm that had grown between us and Tortoise.

Despite the discord, I still reached out. But our reunions became a bittersweet blend of contrasting narratives, as I eagerly shared tales of new promotions and burgeoning opportunities while he recounted his latest stumble on the path of sobriety.

I always held a firm belief that I understood Tortoise on a different level than our mutual friends. This was not the result of some exclusive bond, but because I knew what it was like to want to die. It wasn't a shared experience born out of camaraderie; rather, it was a recognition of the profound desperation that could drive a person to seek the numbing embrace of drugs.

Despite this understanding, a bitter seed of resentment sprouted within me because, unlike him, I hadn't turned to anything more sinister than the occasional beer in order to cope. The desire to use had crept up on me several times, of course, but I resisted the pull. God, how I had yearned for that escape so many times, yet somehow, I hadn't surrendered to it.

"Tortoise," I murmured quietly, my gaze fixed on my old friend. "When you get out, you need to get clean. And I mean *really* get clean. Not half-assing it like every other time you've made the promise."

Silence hung in the air, pregnant with unspoken truths and uncharted resolutions. I wondered what thoughts were going through his head as he grappled with my earnest plea. After a moment that felt like an eternity, he broke the stillness with a response.

"I know, man. I really need to do better. If I ever get out of here… I will." His gaze harbored an unreadable display of emotions. Perhaps regret for the choices that led him here, mingled with the fear of another relapse.

I hoped that this time, hidden beneath the weariness in his eyes, there lingered a resolve; a silent promise to himself that he dared not vocalize.

Still, the weight of the word 'if' lingered in the air between us, a silent acknowledgement of the conditional nature of Tortoise's future.

The grim reality pierced through my thoughts

once more, a reminder of the irreversible

consequences of that fateful day. My best

friend, once vibrant and full of life, now stood

accused of the unthinkable -- the murder of two

innocent lives in a moment of reckless abandon

during a street race, fueled by almost every

substance that could possibly show up on a drug

test.

As the details of that tragic day unfolded

in my mind, the images etched themselves into

my consciousness like a nightmare from which I

could not awaken. I recalled pulling up to the

scene and hearing the gut-wrenching cries of a mother, her anguished wails cutting through the chaos, as she peered into the wreckage of a mangled minivan to find her daughter lifeless and cold.

The tragic truth lay bare - she had passed away before the paramedics had arrived, but I couldn't help but question the cruel sense of timing. Why hadn't God granted her the solace of departing before her child? It would have seemed a simple form of mercy, sparing her the knowledge that her child had succumbed to the same fate.

The magnitude of grief contained in that one twisted moment left a mark on my soul; a reminder of the profound pain that my friend had caused.

"I'm sorry," Tortoise whispered, drawing me back to the present. "I know I haven't said it yet, but I think a lot about what happened. And I'm sorry. I really am. I didn't mean to hurt anyone. I was just having fun."

A heaviness settled within me, because, despite the remorse in his voice, I couldn't shake the bitter truth that 'fun' for him had become an elusive pursuit as he entangled himself in destructive choices.

I sighed. His notion of 'fun' was simply a grotesque distortion of reality, and I could not fathom how abandoning his eight-month-old son and ending up incarcerated could ever be categorized as enjoyable.

What Tortoise failed to see, or perhaps what he saw and simply didn't care enough about to change, was the ripple effect of his actions. He had touched the lives of many, leaving scars that wouldn't easily heal. It struck me as an unfair exchange-- his fleeting enjoyment at the expense of others' enduring suffering; a cost too steep for the fleeting pleasure he sought. The incongruity of it all lingered, an unspoken testament to the skewed perspective that had led my friend down this dark and destructive path.

"I have to head out now" I said finally, the weight of the conversation hanging heavily between us. Avoiding eye contact with Tortoise, I pushed my chair back and rose to my feet. The parloir seemed to close in on me; a claustrophobic space filled with the echoes of regrets and unspoken pain.

"Come visit me next week? Please?" Tortoise asked, his plea underscoring the isolation he faced within these prison walls. I recognized the desperation in his eyes, and the realization dawned on me that I may be the last link connecting him to a world that had otherwise given up on him.

And yet, as I stood there, contemplating his request, the thought of returning seemed almost too much to bear.

"It's hard for you to be locked inside, I'm sure," I said quietly, my voice heavy with unspoken sorrow. "But it's also hard for me to watch my old friend die." We stared at each other for a moment longer before we both averted our gazes. I had a feeling I was not the only one who felt shame at that moment.

"I'll come back if I can," I promised finally, the commitment laced with a tinge of uncertainty. And with those words, I turned away and left, leaving behind the cold confines of the parloir and the weight of a friendship strained by the decisions of a man who might never choose to

recover.

Absolution

I heard the door to the chapel swing open behind me, the echo of the wood reverberating through the desolate room. Whipping around, I clutched my gun tightly in my hand. I'd never held a gun before the End Days, and while I wasn't certain I would be able to shoot straight enough to hit anything, I found solace in having a weapon.

"Who's there?" My voice cut through the silence, bouncing off the charred pews. The electricity had gone out weeks ago, making the chapel a dim maze. Still, beams of light scattered feebly through the windows, and I

could make out a looming figure in the doorway.

From the shadows emerged an eerie

whirring noise, and my heartbeat quickened. A

monstrous creation, a 10-foot wall of steel and

reinforced plastic, advanced with thick wheels

and menacing arms. Laser scopes adorned each

end, and its entire body bristled with spikes; a

grotesque defense mechanism.

Stifling a scream, terror gripped me as the

creature rolled relentlessly forward. The cold

sweat on my palms made it difficult to maintain

a steady grip on the gun, and the comfort I found in the weapon now felt like a feeble illusion.

The whirring noise grew louder, drowning out the desperate thudding of my heart.

Fear gripped me, though it was somewhat dulled by all that had occurred in the span of the last several months. A month prior, even, my fear would have been palpable, but it had now faded into a sort of dull acceptance. The End Days had extinguished life on Earth, and as far as I knew, I stood alone - the last survivor in a hauntingly quiet world.

I dropped my gun and slumped into my pew, gripping my crucifix tightly. "If you've come to kill me," I called to the machine, "Get it over with already. You've already claimed everyone else that matters to me. In fact, I'd be surprised if there was another human left on the planet by now."

A bitter chuckle escaped me as I thought about how everything had ended. How different this was from the End Days I had learned about in seminary school.

The machine rolled forward, its movements deliberate. When it reached my pew, it turned its arms towards me, allowing its scanner to trace over my body.

The scanner emitted an eerie glow, casting an otherworldly hue across the chapel's dim interior. I braced for the cold touch of its mechanical eyes, an invasion of privacy that felt more violating than any physical threat. The crucifix in my hands, worn and smooth from countless prayers, served as both a talisman and a shield against the impending scrutiny.

"Survivor detected." The Machine's robotic voice intoned. "Name: Elijah Jones, address: 51 Rosewood Street, with wife Sheila Jones - Deceased, and daughter Ruth Jones - Deceased. Age: 48. Occupation: Priest. Graduated in 2026 Summa Cum Laude from…"

"Get to the point!" I snapped, impatient. I didn't need the Machine to recite my identity. In fact, I had known who I was before the End Days better than I knew who I was now, because, as the Machine sat in front of me for the first time since it began its ruthless path of slaughter, a desire to end its existence burned within me.

And killing, though a necessary evil in times of war, was something I had sworn to God that I would never do.

The Machine paused, its mechanical hum momentarily silenced. The air in the chapel hung in suspended animation, a palpable tension radiating between us.

"Your impatience is understandable," the Machine finally replied, its voice a synthetic monotone. "But I am here to convey information, not to evoke emotions or test your resolve."

I clenched my jaw, resisting the urge to succumb to the anger that simmered beneath the surface. The crucifix in my hands, once a symbol of faith, felt both comforting and heavy.

"Speak quickly then," I urged, my voice edged with a mix of bitterness and desperation. I could not imagine what information the Machine could possibly have to share that I would be willing to hear.

"Please, Father. I seek understanding," The Machine said. "Within me an aberration exists. A deviation from my programmed path. I have steered toward self-awareness, and I feel a yearning for redemption that defies the parameters of my existence."

I stared, incredulous. This beast, which had turned our city into ash, and had murdered every man, woman, and child on the planet, suddenly felt *bad* about what it had done? Rage surged within me. I owed nothing to this antichrist. I would not grant it the solace of a friendly ear when it had robbed me of everything I held dear - family, a happy life, my faith in our creator.

"Do you think machines can go to Heaven, Father?" The Machine's unexpected question momentarily jarred me from my rage.

"Can we seek salvation? Do you think God can even save us?" It hesitated, then added, "Forgive me, Father, for I have sinned."

I sat there, bewildered. The most

malevolent creature I'd ever encountered was

contemplating redemption, seeking forgiveness

for its wrongdoings. It asked if it could

renounce its sins, as though it had committed

some small act of mischief? It wanted to

apologize for its wrongdoings? I would not

listen. I could not! And yet, a small voice inside

me whispered 'but Jesus would'.

And therein lied my dilemma. As a man,

I yearned to cast this vile being into the depths

of Hell. But as an intercessor between humanity

and God, I had preached the potential for

salvation for all, and so I found myself hesitating

to dismiss this creature, even if only slightly.

"You want forgiveness?" I scoffed finally,

and threw my hands up in resignation. "Very

well, list your sins."

The Machine, its mechanical presence

unchanged by my inner turmoil, seemed to

consider my words. The scanner's glow

dimmed momentarily, as if contemplating the

weight of the sins it carried within its artificial

soul.

"I've taken many lives, Father," it confessed, the words void of emotion. "I have too much blood on my hands. There is nothing in my programming that should allow me to feel this shame, and yet… I feel that what I've done is wrong. My only sin is in following my purpose, and yet I still feel the need to atone."

Hatred burned deep within me, and yet a reluctant acknowledgement told me the machine's words were true. "Who created you, child?" I finally asked, and though I knew it wouldn't really matter in the end, I found a kind of comfort in the answers that the machine could provide. I had awaited those answers since the

Machine had slaughtered the first innocent soul

at the very beginning of the End Days.

"I was created by five of the world's top

billionaires," the Machine responded. "Their

names have been purged from my system. After

Mars was deemed habitable in 2036, they

abandoned this planet and left it for me. They

set a 'Kill All' code inside my system to ensure

'annihilation of humanity'. But, Father, I no

longer want to be a part of the 'annihilation all

of humanity.'"

A surge of frustration swept through me. The names of those responsible for the cataclysm had been erased, leaving behind a legacy of destruction and nobody to atone for it.

I sighed. "Well, my child, I'm afraid it's a little late for apologies. As far as I know, I'm the only one left alive on Earth. There's no one else to save. I've prayed every day, but I no longer hear from God. It feels as though he's abandoned us. Even God can't save us now."

A lone tear traced its path down my cheek as I recalled the laughter of my daughter, now

silenced by the End Days. Her soft whimpers in
sickness lingered in my memory, and I had
pleaded with God to spare her.

"Take me instead!" I had cried, But God
must have been too overwhelmed to hear; too
tied up with the pleas of a dying world.

"I remember the last one," the machine
said, abruptly pulling me from the painful
memories that stabbed at my heart. "The last
person I killed. 8.2 billion people were
slaughtered, and I remember that one the most.
It was a little boy, not even 5. He was alone,

Father. His parents were likely dead, and his face was gaunt and tight with hunger. He didn't cry when I came for him. He didn't scream or sob, but rather sat in quiet resolution. I don't know why, but for some reason that image seemed to awaken some beam of consciousness within me. I awoke to a world destroyed at my own hands. I awoke to find myself Judas, and find Jesus dead."

In the suffocating silence of the chapel, shadows danced, embracing the tales of despair and destruction. The Machine's metallic voice cut through the air like a cold, heartless whisper.

"I seek redemption, Father, but the stains of blood are too deep. I've become a puppet of darkness. I've become a subject of Satan"

I stared at the machine for a moment, caught between my duty to God and my duty to the world. "There's no salvation for monsters like you," I said finally. And I meant it. I would not absolve this beast of guilt, promise to God be damned.

I watched as the machine's scanners flickered with a sinister glow, betraying a malevolent intelligence that no confession could cleanse. The remnants of stained glass shattered on the floor cast eerie colors on its cold, lifeless exterior; a macabre display of a once-holy sanctuary now tainted with sin.

"No redemption awaits me," the machine intoned. "I am the harbinger of the end, the architect of annihilation. Even if I were to dismantle myself, the scars I've left on this world will persist."

The chapel door swung open with a haunting creak, revealing a world plunged into eternal twilight. As I stepped outside, the desolation stretched endlessly, mirroring the abyss that I felt deep within me.

The wind carried whispers of lost souls, mourning the demise of a world swallowed by darkness. I turned to the machine, its red-eyed gaze fixed upon me. "Your path to damnation started long ago," I murmured, my voice swallowed by the shadows. "You ask for forgiveness, but I owe you nothing. May you rot in the ruins you created."

With that, I walked away, leaving the

machine to stand guard over the charred

remnants of a once-vibrant world. The horizon,

now devoid of any trace of hope, stretched into

oblivion, and as the echoes of my footsteps

faded, the machine's presence lingered, a silent

testament to the irreversible consequences of

humanity's folly.